SIMON & SCHUSTER BOOKS FOR YOUNG READERS
Simon & Schuster Building, Rockefeller Center
1230 Avenue of the Americas, New York, New York 10020

SIMON & SCHUSTER BOOKS FOR YOUNG READERS
is a trademark of Simon & Schuster.

Designed by Vicki Kalajian.
The text of this book is set in 22 pt. Bembo.
The illustrations were done in watercolor and colored pencil.
The display type was hand-lettered by Jürg Obrist.

Manufactured in Singapore.

10   9   8   7   6   5   4   3   2   1

*Library of Congress Cataloging-in-Publication Data*
Sonnenschein, Harriet.   Harold's hideaway thumb / by Harriet Sonnenschein ;
illustrated by Jürg Obrist.   Summary: By being diligent
and remembering that he is a big bunny now, Harold succeeds
in stopping sucking his thumb.   [1. Thumb sucking—Fiction.
2. Rabbits—Fiction.]   I. Obrist, Jürg, ill.   II. Title.
PZ7.S699Hap   1991   [E]—dc20   91-6486   CIP   AC
ISBN: 0-671-73568-3

# Harold's Hideaway Thumb

by Harriet Sonnenschein · Illustrated by Jürg Obrist

SIMON & SCHUSTER BOOKS FOR YOUNG READERS
Published by Simon & Schuster
New York · London · Toronto · Sydney · Tokyo · Singapore

When Harold was still a little
bunny, he did the kinds of things
that most other little bunnies do.

At mealtime Harold would sit in his high chair and try to feed himself with his own special spoon. He drank every last drop of milk from his bottle, then threw the bottle onto the floor when he was done.

When Mother took him outdoors, Harold would sit in his stroller and suck contentedly on his thumb.

But with each passing day, Harold grew older and bigger, and as he did, he started acting more and more like the big bunny he was becoming.

When Harold was able to get more food into his mouth than onto the floor, Father suggested that Harold join his parents at the table. Father showed Harold how to drink from a cup. Soon after, Harold decided to throw away his bottle for good.

When Harold got too big for
his little crib, Mother bought him
a big bed.

And it wasn't long before Harold preferred to hop alongside Mother when they went outside.

Mother wondered when Harold would stop sucking his thumb. But that was one thing from Harold's little bunny days that was just too hard for him to give up.

One day, Mother spoke up. "For goodness' sake, Harold," she said, "you're a big bunny now. When will you ever stop sucking your thumb? One of these days I might just hide it from you."

"Maybe then I will forget all about sucking it," thought Harold. He decided to think of some good hiding places.

He hid his thumb between two pages of his picture book. But as soon as he turned the page, Harold put his thumb right back into his mouth.

Harold tried to hide his thumb
in a mitten, but when he took the
mitten off to wash up for dinner,
Harold started to suck his thumb
again without even realizing it.

Finally Harold hid his thumb in his very best hiding spot, the clothes hamper. When Father emptied the hamper, out slid Harold along with all the dirty clothes. His thumb was still hidden, of course—hidden in Harold's mouth!

Harold didn't know what to do. He was sure that no matter how hard he tried, his hideaway thumb would always manage to find its way back into his mouth.

The very next day, at a friend's birthday party, Harold lost his turn because he was sucking his thumb while his friends played Pin the Tail on the Bunny.

Harold left the party with a balloon tied around his wrist. When he moved his hand to get his thumb into sucking position, the balloon bumped him on the nose. "Hmmm," thought Harold. "This balloon just reminded me *not* to suck my thumb."

At home Harold asked Father to help him find other reminders. Father tied a bell to Harold's thumb. The bell would ring if he moved his thumb toward his mouth.

At dinner Harold wore a big red ribbon around his thumb. The ribbon would reach his mouth before his thumb could.

Harold drew pictures of himself sucking his thumb. He hung one in every room of the house.

That way, no matter where he was, there would always be a reminder close by.

One day, Harold overheard Mother and Father talking. "You know," said Mother, "I haven't seen Harold suck his thumb in a very long time. I think that he has finally forgotten all about it."

"Not forgotten," said Harold proudly. "I have remembered. I have remembered that I am a big bunny now."